W9-BRE-022

I'll shake and stir and mix and beat
and make a cake that's yum.

SHAKE, SHAKE, STIR, STIR, MAKE A CAKE THAT'S YUM!

I'm a hungry dinosaur
with cake mix for the pan.

I'll tip it in and pat it down
and smooth it best I can.

TIP, TIP, PAT, PAT, AND SMOOTH IT BEST I CAN!

I'm a hungry dinosaur
I'm hungry for some cake.

I'll slide it in the oven now
and sit and watch it bake.

SLIDE, SLIDE,
SIT, SIT,
SIT AND
WATCH IT BAKE!

I'm a hungry dinosaur
mmmm, the lovely smell.

I'll ice the top and slip and slop
and sprinkle it as well.

SLIP, SLIP, SLOP, SLOP, AND SPRINKLE IT AS WELL!

I'm a hungry dinosaur,
oh, the cake looks nice.

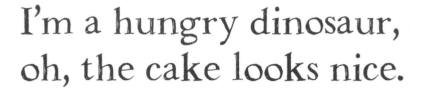

I'll chomp and chew
a piece or two . . .

maybe one more slice!

CHOMP, CHOMP,
CHEW, CHEW,
MAYBE ONE
MORE SLICE!

I'm a hungry dinosaur
I really love to bake.

I think I'll grab my bowl and spoon and . . .

make another cake!

MIX, MIX,
BEAT, BEAT,
MAKE ANOTHER
CAKE!